THE DARKEST HOUR

MIRKA
THE ICE HORSE

With special thanks to Troon Harrison

For Jacob and Eli

www.beastquest.co.uk

ORCHARD BOOKS
Carmelite House
50 Victoria Embankment
London EC4Y 0DZ

A Paperback Original
First published in Great Britain in 2013

Beast Quest is a registered trademark of Beast Quest Limited
Series created by Beast Quest Limited, London

Text © Beast Quest Limited 2013
Inside illustrations by Pulsar Estudio (Beehive Illustration) © Beast
Quest Limited 2013. Cover by Steve Sims © Beast Quest Limited 2013

A CIP catalogue record for this book is available from
the British Library.

ISBN 978 1 40832 400 4

5 7 9 10 8 6

Printed and bound by CPI Group (UK) Ltd, Croydon, CR0 4YY

MIX
Paper from
responsible sources
FSC® C104740

The paper and board used in this book are made from wood
from responsible sources.

Orchard Books is an imprint of Hachette Children's Group
and published by The Watts Publishing Group Limited,
an Hachette UK company.

www.hachette.co.uk

Mirka
The Ice Horse

by Adam Blade

ORCHARD

THE ICY DESERT

KAYONIAN MARSHLANDS

MEATON

THE CITY

ERRINEL

Dear Reader,

My hand shakes as I write. You find us in our hour of greatest peril.

My master Aduro has been snatched away. The kingdom is on its knees. Not one, but two enemies circle our shores – Kensa, the banished witch, has returned from Henkrall. With her stalks Sanpao, the Pirate King. Strange magic is afoot, stirring not just in Avantia but all the kingdoms, and I sense new Beasts lurking.

Only Tom and Elenna stand in the way of certain destruction. Can they withstand the awful test that will surely come? This time, courage alone may have to be enough.

Yours, in direst straits,

Daltec the apprentice

PROLOGUE

Princess Esmeralda stood at the stern
of the flying pirate ship. She tugged on
the rope that bound her wrists and cut
into her skin. The complicated knots
tying the rope to the railing held fast.
*Even if I broke free, where could I go? I'm
trapped on this ship!* Esmeralda stared at
Kayonia speeding by below.

Something strange was happening.
Parts of the kingdom that were usually
far apart were moving closer together.
Where Esmeralda should have seen

cornfields, she saw Kayonia's Icy Desert. Its black sands, whipped by chill wind, rose in glittering clouds. Straining against the ropes, Esmeralda pulled her riding cloak closer about her body.

Perhaps the pirates were behind all this. But no – they didn't wield such power. The strange woman, Kensa, perhaps? She seemed to be the captain's friend. Was she some sort of witch? Dread shivered up Esmeralda's spine. She thought of her mother, Queen Romaine. *Will she be able to rescue me?* For the first time in her life, doubt plunged through her heart.

Esmeralda turned and watched the activity on the deck. A grizzled pirate stood at the wheel, steering northwards with the sun behind his shoulders. Other pirates clung to the rigging and adjusted the sails.

"Tighten that jib!" roared one pirate. "It's flapping like a gossip's tongue!"

Four men sat near Esmeralda, playing cards. They cowered as Kensa strode past, her hair whipping around her face. Strange patterns of wheels and cogs decorated her dark, swirling cape.

Kensa waved the skeleton arm that she carried. Its twisted yellow bones ended in lethal barbs. The pirates cowered lower as though they were going to be lashed.

"You're as scared as kittens!" Kensa sneered. "Just because of the mythical Skeleton Claw!"

As Kensa strode on, the pirates exchanged resentful looks, then continued their game. A young man with plaited blond hair gave a holler.

"You're a dirty cheating dog!" he said.

"So what if I am?" replied a pirate with

a wooden leg. "You're a pudding head!"

The young pirate shoved him in the chest and he fell over backwards. His wooden leg clattered against the deck.

"What's going on?" thundered Sanpao, the captain, leaping up through a hatch, his oiled plait glistening. Esmeralda cowered back, even though she knew he wasn't coming for her.

"No fighting amongst the crew!" Sanpao roared. "We're on a mission to conquer kingdoms. Don't get distracted by petty arguments."

"But this louse was cheating," said the young man.

"You're playing cards with pirates," replied Sanpao. "You didn't expect them to play fair, did you?"

"But—"

Sanpao lunged and grabbed the pirate's blonde pigtail. Then he swung

the man off his feet. Esmeralda jumped
back, jerking her rope tight. Sanpao
heaved the pirate overboard.

With a wail of terror, the man
plummeted towards the icy desert, his
red scarf flapping. Hitting the ground,
he sprawled motionless.

"You've killed him!" Esmeralda said.

"He squeaked like a bilge rat,"
Sanpao sneered and walked to
the wheel. "Prepare to tack!"

With a creak of timbers, the huge ship shifted in the wind.

Esmeralda kept her gaze fixed on the ice. The young pirate twitched and sat up. The fall hadn't killed him! Esmeralda's relief only lasted for a heartbeat, then she saw something strange.

A creature was crossing the ice, taller than any horse Esmeralda had seen. Muscles bulged on its shoulders. Pale blue patterns covered its white coat like shadows on a snowdrift. With sweeping strides, the Beast moved towards the fallen pirate. Spouts of orange flame blasted from its nostrils with every step.

Squinting, Esmeralda saw that the creature's blue hooves were rimmed with claws that helped it balance its weight over the ice. A high-pitched chime rang out, coming from the creature's tail as it swung through the air. Its glittering mass was made up of thousands of icicles, sharp as daggers.

"Sanpao, show mercy!" the pirate cried. "I'll swab decks, anything!"

"We have to throw him a rope!" Esmeralda said.

The hideous creature raised its tail high and whipped it around. Shards of ice shot from it and slammed around the fallen man. Frozen chips burst from the ground, then knitted together around the pirate, forming a cage.

Sanpao and Kensa stood at the rail and watched. "He's trapped like a fish in a barrel," laughed Sanpao.

"Mirka the Ice Horse shows no mercy," Kensa sneered.

Fog drifted between the ship and the ground. Esmeralda stared into the white blanket, her heart hammering. What was happening in her peaceful kingdom?

CHAPTER ONE

CHASING THE ENEMY

"Your Majesty, you look unwell," said Tom.

Queen Romaine had started to sway. Tom and Elenna helped her to her throne. Servants were clearing away the furniture that had been smashed in the fight with Sanpao's pirates.

"This is more than I can bear," the Queen said, tears streaking her face.

"Esmeralda is all I have in the world, and those murderous pirates have taken her."

Tom had never seen Queen Romaine like this. She'd always been so strong.

"Stay calm," Elenna said, patting the queen's armoured shoulder.

People jostled through a door at the end of the room, led by a general in a stiff green uniform. Courtiers in billowing robes clustered behind him.

"Here come your military advisors," Tom said. He and Elenna stepped away from the throne as the general marched closer.

"Your most gracious majesty," he said. "I have never in my long and famous career had to battle with sea scum!"

"But you are my top strategist," murmured the Queen. "Tell me, what do we do now?"

The general's glance fell to the ground.

"The cavalry must ride hard across Kayonia, chasing the pirates' flying ship!" suggested another man.

"But how can we bring the ship down and still save Esmeralda?" asked a woman.

The general glared around.

He doesn't like people telling him what to do, Tom realised.

The Queen's eyes were still trained on her most trusted advisor.

"The matter is simple," the general said. "We go after the ship and fire cannon at its timbers."

Tom frowned. "They'll never be able to drag heavy cannon fast enough to catch up to Sanpao's ship," he muttered.

"And Sanpao will fly higher to avoid the shots," said Elenna.

Soldiers and courtiers began to

argue. Queen Romaine looked paler and more worried than before.

This is a waste of time, Tom thought. *We have a Quest to complete.*

Sanpao the Pirate King and Kensa the Evil Witch were sailing farther away with every passing moment. And more evil was on the loose too. Tom and Elenna's use of the Lightning Path had yielded terrible consequences. New Beasts, once safely imprisoned in their lightning prisons by Tom's father, Taladon, had been released. Their powers were a threat not just to Avantia, but Gwildor and Kayonia too.

"We'll have to rescue Esmeralda ourselves," Elenna said as the advisors continued arguing. "But we must complete our Quest soon."

"Yes," Tom agreed. "I'm worried about Aduro's fate."

After helping them travel to Henkrall by the Lightning Path, Aduro had been taken captive by the mysterious Circle of Wizards. He would only be released if Tom and Elenna brought Kensa to justice.

Hefting his shield, Tom turned towards the door.

"Wait!" Elenna said. "What's happening now?"

They watched as soldiers dragged a man with shaggy hair towards the throne. When he bowed, the metal tools poking from his pockets clanked together.

"Wonderful news, Your Majesty!" the man said. His grinning face was smeared with oil.

"What do you want, Dok?" the Queen asked wearily.

"I have an idea for how we might

rescue Esmeralda!"

A courtier threw an arm around
Dok's shoulder. "Just what we need!"
he said sarcastically. "A crackpot
scientist!"

"Exactly!" Dok nodded
enthusiastically. "Come and see
what I have in my lab."

A groan rose from the crowd.

We need all the help we can get, Tom thought. He stepped forward and raised his voice. "Good people of Kayonia, let's give Dok a chance to share his idea."

"This seems like our last hope," Queen Romaine said, rising from her throne to address the frowning faces in her throne room. With Elenna beside her, she followed Tom and Dok through the palace.

In a courtyard outside, Storm and Silver trotted forward. Tom and Elenna paused to stroke them before hurrying after Dok. Soldiers and courtiers crowded behind as Dok led the way inside an old stable.

Tom blinked as his eyes adjusted to the gloom.

"My extraordinary, fabulous,

stupendous flying machine!" Dok waved at a canvas sheet draped over something lumpy.

"Please, we're in a hurry," Tom said.

The inventor snatched the canvas aside. There was silence as everyone stared.

Dok's invention was a giant, woven wicker cart without wheels. Heavy ropes led from the wicker to a pile of yellow fabric lying on the floor.

The scientist pounced on a corner of fabric and held it up. "Lightest and strongest of all material," he said. "The rare silk woven by Kayonian cave spiders!"

Queen Romaine started in surprise. "So fabric can be woven from the webs!" she said. "I always wondered if this was possible."

"But what does all this do?" Tom asked.

"Aha!" Dok grinned and sprang into the wicker basket. He pointed at a large barrel in one corner. "This is filled with swamp gas from the marshes," he explained. "When I turn this valve, the gas flows through this tubing, and into these burners."

Dok pointed to jets held above his head on a metal framework. "When I strike a spark, the gas catches light. My silk fills with the hot air rising from the flame. And then – we're aloft, we're airborne, we're sailing the wide blue yonder."

Elenna gasped. "This contraption *flies*?"

"On swamp gas?" Tom shook his head in amazement. "It's unbelievable!"

"Believe it, young man!" said Dok, his hair flapping as he clumsily clambered out of the cart.

"If this thing really works, we might have a chance at rescuing Esmeralda," Elenna said.

"Can you show us how to fly it?" Tom asked.

"I can do better than that," Dok said. "I shall accompany you both – as your pilot!"

Tom glanced at Elenna and she gave a worried frown. *This Quest is already complicated,* Tom thought. *I'm not sure we need a mad inventor tagging along.*

"Remember, I am the only one who knows the vessel," Dok said. "You won't get off the ground without me."

"You're right," Tom agreed reluctantly. "Let's get it outside."

Soldiers dragged the wicker vessel into the courtyard. Dok fiddled with valves and taps. There was a hiss of swamp gas and a smell of wet grass.

Dok used a flint to strike a spark. The gas ignited with a roar. Flames shot from the burners.

Courtiers stumbled back with exclamations.

"So bright and hot!"

"It's like dragon's breath!"

But Tom grinned. *This might just work!*

The four balloons rose into the sky, swelling with hot air.

"This is a new way for us to travel!" Elenna said as she and Tom clambered into the basket beside Dok.

"Please look after Storm and Silver," Tom asked Queen Romaine. At that moment, the wolf rushed across the courtyard and leapt into the basket.

"You're so brave!" Elenna said, sounding delighted.

Dok scowled. "I cannot concentrate

when I'm being jumped upon," he said.

Silver let out a long howl.

Dok clapped his hands over his ears. "Make the noise stop and he can stay."

Elenna laid a hand on Silver's head and the wolf calmed down at once.

"Just look after Storm, then," Tom said to the Queen.

"Certainly," said Romaine. "That's a small price for the return of my daughter."

Dok's hands flew amongst the ropes and levers. With a lurch, the basket left the ground and climbed upwards.

"We need to go north," Tom said. "That's where Sanpao's ship was last headed."

As Dok adjusted their course, Tom unfurled his magic map and tried to hold it flat in the gusts of wind. To the north, the map showed the black waste of the Icy Desert. A name wrote

itself across the sand.

"Mirka," Tom read aloud. He turned
to Elenna. "It must be the next Beast."

"I wonder what will happen first,"
Elenna said. "Will we catch up to
Sanpao – or meet our new foe?"

CHAPTER TWO

KNOCKED OUT COLD

As the cart moved through the air, it swayed in the wind.

"We need to balance it out!" Tom said to Elenna. "You go that side and I'll go this." The two of them leaned against opposite sides of the cart. Silver lay between them. Wind moaned in the rigging.

Kayonia's grassy hills streaked below.

Soon Tom noticed black ridges of barren sand lying amongst them. The landscape was changing.

"The Icy Desert is meant to be far to the north," Elenna said.

Tom nodded. Like Gwildor, this kingdom was being warped by the power let loose by the Lightning Path. Distant places were moving closer together.

Quickly, the landscape became barren and flat, empty except for black cacti with pale spines. Dark sand swirled in eddies and Tom's cheeks burned with cold. Elenna's nose was glowing pink. The sun dimmed as dark clouds filled the sky. Lightning flickered and, above the roar of Dok's gas burners, Tom heard the boom of thunder.

"We're in for a storm," he said.

"This beauty is built to ride out any weather," Dok said, patting his basket like a proud parent.

The air grew colder still. Tom looked overboard to see that sheets of pale ice now lay between the sand dunes, gleaming in the flashes of lightning. Dok hauled open a canvas bag and yanked out fur coats.

"Bundle up!" he shouted, thrusting his arms into one of them. Tom and Elenna pulled coats on too. Tom traced their route on his map, making sure they kept going in the right direction to meet a Beast.

Dok's hands flew between ropes and valves, making tiny adjustments to keep the cart level. Tools clattered from his pockets onto the floor.

"You must have a lot of practise to be such a good pilot," Tom said.

"Not so," Dok said with a delighted grin. "This is my maiden voyage. Exciting, isn't it?"

"You could call it that," Tom said, sharing an alarmed look with Elenna. A chill of fear crawled over him despite the warmth of the fur coat. Lightning flashed past, so close that Tom smelled sulphur. Winds spun the wicker basket in a circle while Dok worked feverishly at the controls.

This thing is as flimsy as a leaf, Tom thought, seeing Elenna frowning in concern. Silver pressed against her legs, whining uneasily. His whine rose to a growl and he leaped up, placing his front paws on the rim of the basket.

"Trim the ship! Keep her balanced!" said Dok.

Elenna hastily pulled Silver back inside as the cart shot higher on an

air current. Tom peered out past the
balloons to see what had bothered
the wolf.

In the rushing clouds, he glimpsed
a huge shape. Squinting, he made out
sheets of taut sails, and black raking
masts.

"It's Sanpao's ship!" he yelled, his
heart pounding with excitement.

Maybe now they could rescue Esmeralda from her evil kidnappers!

"Can we catch them?" Elenna asked.

"I'll do my best," Dok said, working at his levers to make his flying vessel rise until it was at the same level as the pirate ship.

"See if you can sail in the ship's wake," Tom directed. "Maybe if we approach from the stern, no one will notice us."

"What's your plan for rescuing the princess?" Dok asked.

Tom shrugged. "I don't really have one," he admitted.

Dok's eyebrows waggled in surprise.

"Don't worry," Elenna said. "Tom's great at figuring things out as he goes along."

"Ah, the experimental method," Dok said in approval. "Trial and error!"

"But I do have Elenna's help,"
Tom said, smiling at his friend.

As they sped after Sanpao's galleon,
lightning flashes winked on cannons,
and Tom saw the sweep of the hull as
it moved through the clouds.

"Try to take us closer," he said
to Dok.

"Could be dangerous," Dok
muttered. "We don't want to be
broadsided. That vessel could smash
mine to smithereens."

He frowned, threw more sandbags
overboard, and opened the jets wide.
Huge flames belched out with a roar.
Tom grimaced at Elenna.

"Let's hope they won't hear us over
this storm," he said.

The air swirled in eddies behind
the huge pirate ship. Dok's fragile
cart bobbed around, throwing Tom

sideways. He grunted in pain as his elbow scraped against a metal support. He and Elenna grabbed ropes to steady themselves. Now Tom could hear the creak of timbers in Sanpao's ship.

Suddenly, pirates swarmed along the stern rail, pointing at Dok's vessel.

"We've been spotted," Tom warned, as the pirates began hurling makeshift missiles. A green glass bottle whistled past Tom's ear. A cabbage bounced off the rigging. A blue bottle crashed into the gas burners and fell to the floor of the cart with a dull *thunk*.

Elenna picked the bottle up and flung it back but it fell short. She started to reach for an arrow. Before she could pull one from her quiver, a pirate with a red beard threw a rock.

"Duck!" Elenna shouted.

The rock thudded into Dok's head.

With a look of surprise, their pilot
buckled at the knees. His hands
slipped from the valves. Elenna caught
him and laid him on the floor.

"Tom, he's unconscious," she said.
"It's down to you to keep us airborne!"

CHAPTER THREE

BOARDED!

Tom's mouth was dry and his heart raced as he reached out an uncertain hand. *I should have watched Dok more closely*, he thought, twisting a valve and hoping to slow the rush of gas.

The flying cart pitched through the air, twirling out of control.

Tom braced himself against the cart as Elenna stood beside him, shooting a stream of arrows. The pirates around the stern dodged back and stopped throwing bottles.

"We need more gas!" cried Elenna.

Tom opened a valve. The balloons filled with hot air and the cart shot up almost level with the ship's stern.

"Can you see Esmeralda?" Elenna asked.

Tom pointed to a girl wrapped in a green riding cape. She was bound to the rail with a length of rope around her wrists. Beyond her, Tom glimpsed Sanpao and Kensa wrestling with the ship's wheel.

"Make this old tub move faster!" the witch shrieked over the wind.

"Let out any more sail and the masts will snap!" roared Sanpao.

They're too busy arguing to notice us, Tom thought. *Now's our chance.*

As the cart drew level, Esmeralda

peered over the rail in surprise. Tom put a finger to his lips. He motioned for Esmeralda to raise her arms into the air. The rope between her wrists and the railing stretched tight.

"Elenna," Tom said, "do you think you could hit that rope?"

"I'll try," Elenna said, notching an arrow.

Tom held his breath. The rope was a tiny target, almost impossible for even a skilled marksman to hit. Dok's cart pitched sideways just as Elenna released her arrow. It shot wide and fell away into the rising mist. Tom yanked on ropes and spun a valve.

"Whilst there's blood in my veins, we'll free her," he muttered.

When the cart flew close again, Elenna shot another shaft. Precise

as a knife blade, the arrow sliced
through Esmeralda's ropes.

"You did it!" Tom said.

Elenna flushed with satisfaction.
"Of course. Whilst there's blood in
my veins, my arrows won't let me
down."

The princess grabbed the cut ends of
the rope and worked the knots free.

When the ropes fell from her wrists, Esmeralda swung herself onto the rail, glancing over her shoulder to make sure no one could see her. Fortunately, Sanpao and Kensa were still arguing.

Elenna gasped. "She's going to jump!"

"We need to get closer," Tom muttered. He twirled a valve, and the cart shot upwards until it almost bumped the black hull.

Esmeralda launched herself off the ship. For a moment she soared with arms spread and her cloak flapping. Then she plummeted. Her hand flashed out. She grabbed a loose end of rigging and, with a thump, she swung into the side of the cart. Elenna hauled her onboard to drop beside the groaning Dok.

Tom let out a breath of amazement.

"'You're as brave as your mother,'"
he said.

"You know Queen Romaine?"
Esmeralda asked, sounding surprised.
Silver was licking her face and she
gently pushed him away.

"We promised her that we'd rescue
you," Tom said.

Elenna smiled at her wolf. "It looks
as though Silver's glad to see you
safe."

Esmeralda suddenly shrieked. Tom
jerked his head up to see a pirate leap
from the stern rail. Another pirate,
the one with the red beard, followed.
They swarmed over the craft's rigging,
as agile as monkeys.

"Elenna, keep us flying!" Tom said.

As Elenna reached for the valves,
Tom sprang to the wall of the wicker
cart. Mist swirled. He wondered how

high they were above the ground.

The Judge took Arcta's eagle feather along with my other tokens, Tom reminded himself, knowing that if he fell from the rigging, death was certain.

As the frail craft swayed, he grabbed the rigging and shimmied upwards. His body rocked in the wind and he had to hold on tight, his muscles trembling. *I can do this!*

A black boot swung down and kicked Tom in the shoulder. He managed to reach out to catch the pirate by the leg.

"Get off me, you worm!" the pirate shouted. He grabbed a trailing rope. Wrenching his leg free, he jumped out into the air, then swung back towards Tom in a blur of speed. The sharp edge of his cutlass gleamed.

Tom yanked out his sword and his blade rang against the pirate's weapon.

"Behind you!" he heard Elenna shriek.

Tom spun on the rigging and another cutlass flashed, nicking his neck. He shoved the pirate away with his feet, making the man spin on his dangling rope. Tom thudded back against the rigging.

The pirate swung towards Tom again, his hair streaming away from his tattooed forehead. "Death to Avantians!" he yelled.

Tom yanked himself higher and brought his sword whistling in beneath the pirate's arm. It smacked into the man's wrist and his cutlass went tumbling into the mist. The pirate scrabbled away from Tom.

He heard Dok groaning. He didn't dare glance down. His gaze was fixed on the pirates with their curved blades. Another was descending towards Tom, his eyes blazing. His weapon had three hooked blades, and the pirate's red beard was matted and thickt. On the muscles of his bare

shoulder, a red tattoo of flames and spattered blood surrounded the name Jin.

Tom lowered his sword until it was pointing at Jin's chest. The pirate drew his lips back in a snarl. His teeth were filed into points.

"I'm not afraid of you, Avantian chicken," Jin said.

"And I'm not afraid of you, sea scum," Tom replied.

Suddenly Jin leapt from the rigging, somersaulting in mid-air. His curved blade flashed past Tom's ankles, and sliced open the toe of Tom's boot. Tom scrambled higher as Jin landed on a rope beside him. Clinging with one hand, Tom used his other to slash his sword in a high stroke. Jin swung his own weapon, and hooked one of the curved blades around Tom's sword. The blade slid to the sword hilt in a shower of sparks. Tom felt sweat running down his face as he struggled to free his sword. Jin jumped into the air, almost wrenching Tom's sword from his hand. The pirate leant back, braced against ropes, and jerked harder on Tom's blade.

Tom's muscles bulged as he twisted his sword inside the curved blade. Metal shrieked. Finally Tom hauled his sword free. Jin jumped out of reach and climbed higher.

The balloons surged upwards, passing the huge hull of Sanpao's ship. Tom could see the faces of pirates as they craned to watch.

Silver was whining from the cart below them, clearly anxious about Tom's plight.

"I'm going to enjoy taking you

down," the pirate said. "You're the boy who sneakily defeated Sanpao."

"There was nothing sneaky about the many times I've defeated your captain," Tom replied.

"Is that so?" Jin smirked. "All the pirates of Makai know that Avantians are dirty fighters."

Tom flushed with anger. He scrambled after Jin, slashing his sword wildly. The pirate threw

himself upside down to avoid the blade. For a moment he hung from the rope by his toes. Then he moved sideways, like a spider in a web, and joined the other pirate.

Tom lunged after Jin, still swinging his sword. Its lethal tip ripped open a tear in the yellow silk of the balloon, which sagged as hot air rushed out. Tom felt the ropes tug as the cart beneath him began to sink.

CHAPTER FOUR

A HARD LANDING

"Tom! Get back down here!" Elenna called up to him.

I let my anger get the better of me, Tom thought. *I've ruined Dok's ship, and put my Quest in jeopardy. I've failed!*

"Time to abandon ship!" Jin shouted. He linked hands with the other pirate and they swung outwards on a rope. They landed neatly on the deck of Sanpao's galleon.

"Say hello to Mirka!" Jin called mockingly.

As Dok's vessel plummeted, Elenna's hands flew over levers.

"Tom, I need your help!" she called.

Tom sheathed his sword and swung through the rigging. He glimpsed the icy ground rushing to meet them.

We're not going to live long enough to face Mirka!

"Ow, my head!" Dok groaned. "What's happening?"

"We're going to crash land!" Tom replied.

"Not with my precious vessel you're not," said Dok. The scientist staggered to his feet and peered overboard. His eyes went wide. "Pull this rope – all the way!" Dok said.

Tom rushed to obey.

"Twist this valve!" the inventor

called. As Elenna twisted, Dok heaved
sandbags out. The cart lurched and
rose. It hovered for a moment but
then began whistling down again.
Dok's hands moved swiftly between
ropes and levers.

"Watch out!" Tom called. A dark
dune loomed out of the mist. The
bottom of the cart scraped it, and
Esmeralda tumbled to her knees with
a cry. Cold air rushed past, turning
the sweat in Tom's hair almost to ice.
Droplets of mist clung to every rope
and dripped from the silk balloons.

"Brace yourselves!" Dok
commanded. The cart smacked
against icy ground and skidded across
it. The balloons sank in a smothering
yellow cloud. With a horrible lurch,
the cart flipped onto its side and
threw everyone onto the ice.

The burners went out. In the silence, Tom climbed to his feet with one hand on his sword. Mist swirled around. *Mirka could be right beside us and I wouldn't even know*, Tom thought.

"Is anyone hurt?" Elenna asked.

Dok and Esmeralda stood up, rubbing bruised elbows and knees.

"No broken bones," the Princess said.

"Not my best landing," Dok grumbled.

"Considering you've never flown before, it was a terrific landing!" Elenna said. She smoothed her hands over Silver to make sure he wasn't injured. The wolf's hackles rose. He began sniffing at the ice.

"What is it, boy?" Elenna stared at the tracks scored in the shiny surface.

"Did we make these when we landed?" Tom asked, pointing to the curved scars in a carpet of thin snow.

"I don't think so," Elenna replied. "They look like the tracks of an animal with hooves." Stooping, she followed the markings across a sheet of ice.

"Here, the tracks look like they

were made by claws." Elenna
frowned in puzzlement at the lines
scratched into the ice.

"Maybe they were made by two
different animals," Tom said.

"Or one animal with hooves and
claws," Elenna said. Silver growled
and she laid a hand on his head.
"I didn't expect that."

"The unexpected is just what you
should be expecting on a Beast
Quest!" A familiar voice drifted
from the fog.

Tom spun around. "Daltec, is
that you?"

An image of the young wizard
appeared in the air. His eyes darted
from side to side.

*He's worried about being spied on by
the Circle of Wizards*, Tom realised.

"I wanted to make sure you were

safe," Daltec said. "How fares your
Quest?"

"Kensa and Sanpao are deadly
opponents," Tom replied. "They're
still at large."

"And we haven't found the next
Beast yet," Elenna said.

"I can sense that it's very close," Daltec said. "Beware! Mirka is…" Daltec's image wavered like smoke, and he faded away.

Tom walked to where Dok and Esmeralda were shoving the cart upright again.

"Elenna and I are tracking something," he said. "Can you wait here for us?"

"Fine, fine," Dok said. He was too busy running his hands over the burners to pay much attention to Tom. He tutted, noticing a dent, and reached into his pocket for a tool.

"Repairs to be done," he said. "Princess, will you help by untangling the ropes?"

"Certainly," Esmeralda said. She waved at Tom. "By the time you return, we'll be ready to fly again."

Tom thanked her, before hurrying after Elenna and Silver as they tracked the strange marks over the frozen land.

Just what sort of Beast is Mirka? Tom wondered, his throat tight with fear.

CHAPTER FIVE

A FREEZING PRISON

Silver kept his nose to the ground. On snow, the strange clawed tracks were easy to follow, but where they crossed ice, they were more difficult to see. Fog licked Tom's face. Frost coated Elenna's hair and sparkled in Silver's ruff. Tom's whole body shivered.

"We need to complete this Quest quickly, before the cold kills us all," he said.

"At least we have Dok's fur coats," Elenna replied.

"Yes, but I'm not sure if I can fight so bundled up." *In fact, my fingers are so numb that I can hardly feel them*, Tom thought. *How am I going to grip my sword?*

A bright flash caught Tom's attention. He wondered if it was lightning, but he hadn't heard any thunder for a while and the storm seemed to be over. He stopped and stared into the gloom.

"What's the matter?" Elenna asked.

Tom pointed to the west. For a moment, they both held still, waiting. Just as Tom was beginning to think he'd imagined the light, something tiny – like a flicker of fire – shone and went out. It repeated the pattern once more.

"What can it be?" Elenna asked.

Cautiously they went on, keeping still

when the light vanished and walking towards it when it shone. Silver growled, his hackles rising.

"Look. There's something close by," she whispered. "Something else."

Tom's hand dropped to his sword as he made out bars of ice gleaming through the freezing fog. There was a young man imprisoned inside. "It's an ice cage!"

The prisoner fell to his knees. "P-please, kind st-st-strangers," he said, his teeth chattering with cold. "Help me escape!"

"But what are you doing here?" Tom said.

"My captain threw me overboard," the man said. He drew a red scarf from his face to reveal a tattoo of a Beast skull on his cheek.

"So you're one of Sanpao's thieves," Tom said.

"Free me. I swear on the grave of my
mother not to attack you," the pirate
said, wriggling on the ice. The clang of
metal caught Tom's attention. He stared
at the pirate's hoop earring, heavy
woollen tunic, and canvas trousers –

and then saw what had caused the sound. The pirate was hiding a knife beneath one leg.

"I'm not sure I believe you," Tom said.

"B-but I swear it on the grave of my mother's mother!" cried the pirate.

"This man is going to freeze to death," Elenna said.

Can I trust him? Tom wondered. He hardened his heart. "We'll return soon," he said. "If you're still alive, we'll let you out."

Tom turned his back on the pirate's pleas, and began walking towards the glowing light once more. His hand tightened around the hilt of his sword. *Whatever's waiting for us, I'm ready.*

Elenna fell into step alongside as Tom plunged into the fog. "Are we doing the right thing?" she asked.

"We need to take care of our Quest first," Tom said.

Elenna snatched at Tom's sleeve as the light bobbed on the horizon. "It's started moving!" she whispered.

Tom's eyes strained into the swirling gloom. Flicker. Darkness. Flicker.

Elenna's right – each flicker is bigger than the last! A thrill of dread tingled in Tom's chest. *Maybe the pirate was telling the truth!*

"Let's keep walking," he said, trying to sound braver than he felt.

Tom's boots slipped on the ice. He caught his balance and moved on. There was no sound in the foggy desert.

Then Tom began to hear air whooshing in and out as though something huge was breathing heavily.

"The flame is flickering in time to the breathing," Elenna whispered.

Tom nodded, hairs standing up on his neck. He'd had enough of waiting – he wanted to complete this Quest now.

"Come out and fight us!" he called.

In answer, the dull thud of hoof beats vibrated in Tom's chest.

"It must be Mirka," Elenna said, raising her arrow higher.

But Tom still couldn't see the Beast! He lifted his cold fingers to his mouth and blew on them. They needed to be warm enough to wield his sword when the moment came.

The two of them circled on the spot, inspecting the landscape. Nothing. Only in the distance, the ice cage and, beyond that, the small outline of Dok's cart. Tom's nerves were stretched taut.

The mist was shredded by four massive legs, as tall and thick as oak trunks. Hard blue hooves smashed into a drift of snow. Frozen chunks of ice flew into the air and rained around Tom and Elenna. Mirka's long face was like that of a horse, but featured dark eyes glowing with evil anger. Fire spurted from his nostrils with every breath, and cast an orange sheen over the black ice.

Tom's numb fingers fumbled at his sword hilt as Mirka's pale shoulders emerged from the fog. Bulging slabs of muscle were shadowed with blue patterns. His tangled, icy mane glittered like a deadly wave. The sharp points of spikes, looking like blue icicles, gleamed on Mirka's forehead.

"He's huge!" Elenna gasped as the

Ice Horse loomed closer.

Tom yanked at his blade. "Prepare
to fight with everything you've got!"

CHAPTER SIX

A FIGHT IN THE FOG

Mirka stopped and flung up his head.
His tail, formed of hundreds of sharp
icicles, lashed from side to side. It
made a high-pitched ringing sound.

"He's seen us," Tom said. The Beast's
eyes were trained on his face, boring
into him.

Mirka snorted a blast of flame, rows
of sharp blue teeth visible in his gaping

mouth. A bellow of challenge rang
from deep in his throat.

Tom jumped forwards, his sword
raised high, but his boots slipped
again. The tip of his blade crashed
onto the ice, sending jolts of pain up

his arm. Desperately, Tom struggled to find his balance and raised his sword again. *How are we going to fight if we can't even stand up properly?*

Mirka lowered his head and flattened his ears. He lumbered into a charge. The horn that protruded from his skull was aimed straight at Tom's heart.

Elenna pulled her bowstring taut. Just as she shot an arrow, her feet slipped. The shaft streaked off into the fog.

"I can't do this, Tom," she panted, righting herself. She frowned at the ice. "Something isn't right."

Tom held his sword in front of his chest. Mirka was moments away. Perhaps he could swing his weapon against the underside of Mirka's neck... A waft of hot air blasted Tom's face. The

Beast came closer and closer, vibrating the ice beneath Tom's feet. He got ready to leap to one side and swing his sword at the Beast, but at the last moment Mirka shifted sideways. His mane whipped Tom's cheeks, opening cuts. Pain stung his face.

Tom felt the Ice Horse's huge head slam into his back, sending him flying through the air. He landed face down, pain exploding in his ribs and knees as his sword clanged against the ice. When he pushed himself up, he could see blood from his cheeks staining the ice. He rolled over in time to see Mirka rearing up, his pale belly filling Tom's view. The Beast lashed out with his blue hooves. Tom saw that each hoof was lined with spiky claws.

No wonder Mirka left such strange

tracks, and is so sure-footed on the ice,
he thought.

A grey shape flashed past Tom's eyes
as Silver jumped in between him and
the Beast. He growled a savage threat,
the hairs standing straight up in his
ruff, just as arrows whipped past Tom's
shoulder. They hit the Beast's flanks,
knocking out shards of ice.

Mirka dropped his fore-hooves down
and whirled with teeth bared, ready to
attack Tom's closest friend.

Now's my chance!

Tom stood up as Mirka sent a huge
roar in Elenna's directions. Tom threw
off Dok's fur coat so that he could fight
more easily.

Elenna stood her ground and bravely
shot another arrow at the Beast, but
Mirka snaked out his head and blasted
it with flames. The shaft crumbled

into black ash. Silver leapt forwards,
growling. He jumped at the Beast's
legs but Mirka kicked out sideways.
The blow lifted Silver into the air.
Yelping, he landed hard on the ice.

"Stay away!" Elenna called, as her
wolf scrambled to his paws and limped

out of range of Mirka's clawed hooves. She fumbled to notch another arrow as the Ice Horse charged at her.

"Just run!" Tom shouted. Now that he was back on his feet, he could end this.

He began to run, but his speed was no match for the Beast's long stride. Skidding to a halt, Tom hauled his shield from his back. He planted his feet as firmly as he could, and flung it with all his strength. It whistled through the air in a spinning blur. With a dull thud, it slammed into Mirka's head. The Ice Horse gave a shrill cry. His eyes rolled white and he stopped, giving his dazed head a shake.

Elenna sprinted away with Silver. Tom began running again with his sword raised high. Mirka loomed ahead like a wall of freezing bone and muscle. Tom dropped to his knees, sliding forwards on the ice and snatching up his shield as he passed by. He flashed between Mirka's legs, and underneath the Ice Horse's curving belly. *Perhaps that's the weak spot!* Tom slashed upwards with his sword, scoring wounds in the soft flesh.

Mirka bellowed with pain. Tom shot out the other side, still on his knees. Mirka lashed his tail around, roaring with pain. Tom could see each of the dagger-like teeth in his mighty jaws. Mirka locked eyes with him and whipped around his tail, lined with jagged icicles. Tom raised his shield just in time, but the crunching blow knocked the wind from his chest and sent him sprawling.

Tom gasped for breath. He struggled to stand up as pain throbbed across his body. Through blurred vision, he was dismayed to see that his sword blows had not done much to stop Mirka. The Ice Horse was charging after Elenna again. His claws raked gouges from the ice, and his glittering, spiked mane tossed angrily. Elenna's arrows bounced off his hard shoulders, falling uselessly to the ice.

Suddenly Mirka stopped and reared up. As his fore-hooves slammed to the ground again, he raised his tail above his body. Icicles shot from it in a blue stream. They rained around Elenna. As they hit the ground they sent up sprays of ice crystals. The ice shimmered in the air, then hardened into solid bars.

Another ice cage!

Elenna was completely trapped by ice. Just like the young pirate, Tom's best friend was at Mirka's mercy!

CHAPTER SEVEN

THE CANYON'S EDGE

Tom's heart pounded.

Elenna's eyes were wide as she stared through the cage bars, trying to lever them apart with her hands. Mirka circled the prison, snorting and pawing at the ground. Silver, watching from a distance, raised his muzzle in a terrified howl.

"Help me!" Elenna called. She

bashed at the bars with her bow but the ice didn't yield.

Tom sprinted in a wide circle around Mirka. The Beast wheeled on his hind legs, keeping Tom in his line of sight. Tom could see the light of victory in the Ice Horse's furious eyes – they glowed like dark embers. *Not too fast, Mirka*, Tom thought. *This fight is not over yet.*

He rushed at the cage and hacked at the ice with savage blows. His sword blade rang and shivered as frozen dust sprayed into the air. Elenna continued bashing at the inside. Soon, a network of cracks appeared in the cage's bars.

"Watch out!" Elenna cried.

Tom swivelled to see Mirka's front legs swinging towards him. He hoisted his shield just as the Beast reared, lashing his clawed front hooves. They

smashed into the shield with a mighty
blow. Pain flashed up Tom's arms. He
cried out and staggered back until he
was pressed against the bars of the
cage.

The Beast's front hooves slammed
down only a stride away from Tom's
boots. Mirka stepped back, creating
room for another attack. Behind him,
Tom could hear Elenna chipping

away at the ice with her bow.
Mirka had them both trapped!

The Beast tossed his head and
reared again. His clawed hooves
pawed the air above Tom's head.

"Get out of the way!" screamed
Elenna.

Tom tried to raise his shield but his
arms shook with weakness and pain.
He couldn't heft his shield above
waist-height. As Mirka's hooves
slammed down, Tom dropped to
his knees and rolled sideways. Ice-
dust sprayed over him and the Beast
roared in fury.

He scrambled to his feet, his shield
and sword hanging from his numb
hands. *I need to get away from Mirka
and regain my strength. But how can
I leave Elenna?*

Tom glanced from Mirka, circling

and snorting, to the cage. Elenna pressed her face to a hole and looked out.

"Don't worry about me!" she shouted, even though her lips were blue with cold. "Run, Tom!"

Tom began dragging his feet across the ice. Hoof beats thundered in his head. Risking a glance back, he saw that Mirka was streaking after him. Tom bent his head and pumped his legs. Pain filled his lungs and he gasped for breath. *If only I had the extra speed from the Golden Armour.*

Closer and closer Mirka galloped, and the ground shook under Tom's feet. He felt the singeing flame from Mirka's nostrils just behind him.

Whack! Something hit him in his spine, lifting him from his feet. Mirka had butted his spikes into his back!

His vision filling with writhing
black spots, he crashed onto ice as
smooth as marble. He slid along,
scrabbling with his hands but unable
to stop.

The ground began to drop away
and Tom realised with horror that a
steep canyon was opening up before
him. Tom stuck the point of his sword
into the ice and managed to come to
a stop. He glanced over his shoulder,
muscles screaming with pain.

His jaw dropped in shock.

Just beyond his toes, the ground fell
into a dark chasm. Tom's head swam
dizzily. If his sword came loose from
the ice, he'd plunge to his death.

Then he spotted something else –
a long, narrow bridge of ice crossing
the canyon. It looked almost too
fragile to hold his weight, much

less the weight of a Beast.

A plan began forming in Tom's mind.

Maybe all is not lost yet…

CHAPTER EIGHT

A WILD RIDE

Galloping hoof-beats shook Tom from his thoughts. Mirka was coming for him. The only route of escape lay over the canyon! He rolled over to one side, pulling his sword free. Before he could struggle to his feet, the Ice Horse rushed at him, stamping his hooves madly. Tom jerked his arms and legs, wriggling to get out of the way of the shards of ice attacking him like a small blizzard.

I've got to get up before I'm trampled to death!

Tom lurched onto his knees and rose to his feet. Mirka bucked, twisting his whole body, and let out a roar, his yellow eyes glistening. Crouching and slipping, Tom ran as fast as he could away from the edge of the canyon.

How can I defeat this Beast? he wondered. *I can't let it attack me from the front because of his clawed hooves, and that vicious tail protects his back.*

But there was still that bridge across the canyon... Tom was a good rider and had spent many days on his stallion, Storm. Maybe he could ride Mirka too?

Tom stared into Mirka's fiery eyes. He reached into his tunic and closed his fingers around the ruby jewel, which allowed him to communicate

with Beasts – the one magic token
he'd managed to keep hold of, after
the Judge had stripped him of all his
other powers.

"Steady there, Mirka," Tom
murmured. "Steady."

The Beast paused. *It's working!*

Still, Tom's mouth was dry with fear.
Step by step, he approached Mirka,
whose massive flanks rose and fell
with his steady breathing.

Soon he could almost touch the Ice-Horse's frosty muzzle. Anger flared in the Beast's eyes as he snorted. One blast from those nostrils and Tom would be incinerated.

"Steady there," Tom repeated.

Mirka hesitated, then he lunged forward. His huge teeth snapped at Tom's shoulder, but the moment's pause had given Tom just enough time to leap to one side. He flung himself into the air and snatched at Mirka's glittering mane. He hauled himself onto the Beast's back, ignoring the stinging pain from the icicles.

Mirka bucked, his rear legs kicking the air, his roar as loud as a hundred lions. Tom clung on, his legs slipping on the frosty flanks. The spiky tail lashed at Tom, its icicles ringing. Just in time, Tom flung up his shield for

protection. The deadly tail crashed
against it, jerking Tom's arm.

Mirka bucked and reared up into
the fog, smashing his hooves back to
the ice again. He twisted and thrashed,
lashing out with his front claws. Tom's
grip on his sword weakened. Blood

was seeping from his cuts, freezing against his skin.

Then the world became a blur of fog and flying mane as Mirka spun his body in a tight, fast circle. Tom's head filled with dizzy spots as his sword flew from his hand.

No! Tom thought in dismay. *Now the ice bridge really is my last hope of defeating Mirka.*

Tom battered his shield against Mirka's neck, trying to force him to turn towards the canyon, but the Beast was too powerful and ignored the blows. He arched his back into a bulging mass of muscles and Tom couldn't hold on. He flew through the air and landed with a crash beside his sword. Snatching it up, he climbed shakily to his feet. Every bone in his body screamed for rest.

Mirka lowered his head and charged.

Tom held his sword high, circling. He knew this would be his final stand.

I need a miracle to save me now…

Behind Mirka, something loomed in the sky. Dok's flying vessel! Only three balloons were filled, but it was keeping a fast but lurching course. Tom waved an arm and the Ice Horse skidded to a halt. He narrowed his eyes, as if assessing this new threat. With a roar of gas burners, the cart hovered overhead.

"Do you need some help?" Dok called, peering out.

"I've been trying to ride this Beast!" Tom shouted.

"I can help with that!" Esmeralda snatched up a rope and knotted it into a lasso. She climbed to the edge of the cart, then into the rigging where she clung with one hand. In the other hand, she twirled her rope,

waiting for the right moment. The Ice
Horse reared up, roaring at Dok's cart.
Instantly, Esmeralda flung her rope.
The coil fell neatly around Mirka's
neck. Still holding the other end,
the princess leapt from the craft and
landed astride the Beast. He squealed
and bucked but Esmeralda held on.

Behind her, Tom saw the Beast's spiked tail raise into the air

She doesn't realise! Tom hefted his sword and bounded forward. As Mirka brought his tail down to strike at Esmeralda, Tom hacked at it with his sword, putting all his strength into the strikes and creating sprays of icicles. Mirka roared in fury and pain. Ice scattered everywhere as Tom dealt blow after blow. With the princess on his back, the Beast didn't know whether to stop and attack Tom or try to throw her clear. Tom kept swinging his blade, his shoulders aching as it bit home. Soon Mirka's roars had become low moans, his tail shattered to a useless stump.

Tom was surrounded by shards of ice. He felt a thrill of hope as he looked up at Esmeralda. She was still astride the Beast – just. *At last, the tables have turned.*

CHAPTER NINE

PLUNGING TO CERTAIN DEATH

"There's a canyon ahead of us!" Tom called. "Steer the Beast over there. We need to get Mirka onto that bridge."

Esmeralda made a loop in the end of her rope. She flung it around one of Mirka's ears. Then she hauled it tight, dragging the Beast's head towards the canyon. He roared with rage. But Tom circled the Ice Horse, thrusting his sword, while Esmeralda kept a tight pressure on the rope. Gradually they forced the Beast towards the dark chasm. He seemed too exhausted to put up much of a fight.

"That bridge isn't strong enough to hold Mirka!" Esmeralda called. For the first time, fear showed on her face. "Do you know what you're doing, Tom?'

"No, but that's never stopped me before!" Tom said, grinning. "Jump off before you get hurt."

Tom rushed in front of Mirka and lunged at his head. He kept just out of reach of Mirka's hooves. The Beast charged forwards, angered by the flash of Tom's sword. As the front claw-hooves touched the bridge, Esmeralda leapt off.

Tom backed along the structure. It was only just wide enough for him. On each side, the canyon dropped into a foggy void. Tom couldn't see the bottom. Sweat froze on his forehead as the ice creaked beneath his weight.

Will the bridge hold me long enough to defeat Mirka? Tom had no way of knowing. He could only pace backwards while Mirka stamped after him. The Beast's clawed hooves gripped the bridge far better than Tom's boots, which failed him as he took another step back. His foot shot forward, his

arms windmilling as he fought for balance. Mirka's fiery snort sounded amused. The Beast sensed a victory.

Time to use the Lightning Tokens, Tom thought. He paused in the middle of the bridge and fumbled at his belt. But his bag containing the Lightning Tokens was gone! It must have fallen off in the battle with Mirka.

The Beast began creeping forward. The ice splintered and cracked beneath his massive weight and a quiver ran through the bridge.

Tom held his ground, trembling. *I cannot fail this Quest*, he thought. The safety of the kingdoms, and Aduro's freedom, depended on him.

At that moment, Elenna rushed through the mist behind Mirka, with Silver at her side. She must have managed to free herself from her prison at last. "Do you need this?" she called, waving Tom's bag over her head.

Tom felt a shudder of relief. "Throw me a token – quickly!" he said.

Elenna fumbled in the bag and held aloft a purple Lightning Token. It was glowing, its edges flickering with tiny flames. Elenna hurled it, but her throw was short. Tom watched in horror as it fell towards the ice at Mirka's feet.

I can't reach it...

He shielded his face as the token exploded with a deafening boom. As he lowered his arm, he saw Mirka rearing up, roaring. His hooves wheeled as a network of cracks appeared in the ice – but the bridge still held!

I'll have to take a bigger risk. To crack the ice, I'll need to make the Beast angrier still.

Tom stepped closer to Mirka, and reached for his red jewel. He concentrated his thoughts on getting through to the Beast. But as soon as he touched the ruby, a powerful message assaulted his mind.

The son of Taladon must die!

Tom gripped the jewel more firmly. Each of the Beasts freed from their Lightning Prisons had been driven by the same mad impulse for revenge.

"Come and get me then," Tom said. "I'll make you suffer just like my father did."

Fire blasted from Mirka's nostrils and ice sizzled. The Beast reared up, and Tom skidded backwards to avoid the clawed hooves. He felt his heart beat getting faster as ice shuddered at the edge of the chasm, beneath Mirka's frenzied stamping.

As Tom got to his hands and knees, he heard a low groan that didn't come from any animal. More noises rang through the air, moaning like ghosts.

"It's the ice!" Elenna called. "It's breaking apart."

With a great tearing sound, a portion of the bridge gave way beneath the Beast's clawed hooves. Mirka scrabbled for balance, his eyes rolling with panic. Too late. With an echoing

cry, he plunged over the edge and into
the abyss. His vast, pale body turned
over and over. Tom caught glimpses of
his spiked mane and icy tail. The last
thing he saw was the yellow glow of
Mirka's eyes blinking shut for the last
time as the Beast plummeted down

into the dark chasm. Then the fog swallowed him up.

For a moment, there was silence, until Silver yipped with excitement.

Elenna and Esmeralda cheered. "You did it, Tom," called his friend. "You defeated Mirka!"

Tom climbed to his feet, wincing. His whole body was battered and bruised. Cautiously he began inching back across the bridge, the way he had come. As he reached the shattered portion where Mirka had fallen, a creaking sigh ran through the ice as it shifted beneath his feet. Tom halted, every muscle tense.

With a groan, the bridge fell away. In a spray of flying ice, Tom plunged headfirst into the chasm.

CHAPTER TEN

A THREAT TO AVANTIA

Black ice and smooth rock rushed past. Tom tried to cry out in terror, but the wind tore his breath away. He was helpless without the magical power of Arcta's eagle feather that saved him from high falls – one of the six magical powers the Circle of Wizards had taken away from him.

This is the end of my Beast Quests, Tom

thought, squeezing his eyes shut
and bracing himself for death.

"*Oof!*"

He plunged into something warm
and soft. It billowed around his body
and held him suspended in the air.
Opening his eyes, Tom saw shining
yellow fabric. The roar of gas burners
and the creak of ropes filled the
canyon's silence.

"Ahoy!" yelled Dok. "Climb down,
young man!"

Tom's whole body tingled with relief. His friend had saved him using the flying vessel! The inventor must have steered the cart into the chasm. Tom caught hold of a rope and slid across the balloon before lowering himself into the rigging. He scrambled down and jumped into the wicker cart.

"Dok, you've saved my life!" he said. "And I hadn't even noticed that you were here!"

Dok's wavy hair flapped as he laughed. "I didn't want to miss out on the action between you and the Beast. I glimpsed it all thanks to my marvellous flying contraption."

Tom clapped the inventor on the back. "Take us up, Dok!"

Dok opened the burners wider. The balloons rose until the cart was level

with the lip of the canyon. It landed
bumpily. Silver jumped onboard,
followed by Elenna and Esmeralda.
They both threw their arms around
Tom.

"I thought that was the end,"
Elenna said. "I can't believe you're
safe."

"And you broke out of the ice
cage!" Tom said.

"Yes," Elenna agreed. "I freed the
pirate from his cage too."

"Did he threaten you?"

"No!" Elenna laughed. "He was
more interested in stealing your
abandoned fur coat than in fighting
me."

"Don't worry about the coat," Dok
said. "I'm experimenting with fabric
that grows its own fur." He heaved
sandbags overboard. "Setting course

for Meaton," he said. "Let's take
you home, Princess."

As they rose from the ice, Tom
craned his neck for a last glimpse of
the canyon. Its ribbon of darkness was
Mirka's final resting place.

Another Beast had been vanquished.

Tom must have slept for the whole
journey, because when he woke the
basket was landing in the courtyard
of Queen Romaine's palace.

"Where are we?" Elenna mumbled,
rubbing her eyes.

"Home!" Esmeralda bounced from
the cart as her mother ran over the
cobbles. She clasped Esmeralda in
a tight hug.

"I've been so worried about you!"
she said.

"My friends rescued me from the pirates!" Esmeralda explained, and the Queen stepped forward to shake hands with Dok, Tom, and Elenna. Esmeralda gave Tom a smile.

"You must stay here and tonight we'll celebrate with a feast," Queen Romaine said.

Tom and Elenna glanced at each other. The offer was tempting but there were still enemies loose in the kingdoms.

"Thank you," Tom said. "But our work isn't finished yet."

"There's something I must tell you," Esmeralda said, stepping closer so that the courtiers couldn't hear. "When I was Sanpao's captive, I overheard something. Kensa and Sanpao made plans to launch a strike on Avantia very soon."

"Avantia?" Elenna gasped.

"There is not a moment to lose!" Tom said. "We must head home right away and fight for our kingdom!'

"Yes," Elenna agreed. "Let's find Storm."

As they rushed to the stables, followed the whole way by a

scampering Silver, troubles clouded Tom's heart. This was worse than anything he could have predicted. If Kensa and Sanpao travelled to Avantia, there was no telling what death and destruction they would take with them.

This Quest had just become personal.

Join Tom on the next stage
of the Beast Quest when he meets

KAMA
THE FACELESS
BEAST

Win an exclusive
Beast Quest T-shirt and goody bag!

Tom has battled many fearsome Beasts and we want to know
which one is your favourite! Send us a drawing or painting of
your favourite Beast and tell us in 30 words why you think
it's the best.

Each month we will select **three** winners to receive
a Beast Quest T-shirt and goody bag!

Send your entry on a postcard to
BEAST QUEST COMPETITION
Orchard Books, 338 Euston Road, London NW1 3BH.

Australian readers should email:
childrens.books@hachette.com.au

New Zealand readers should write to:
Beast Quest Competition, PO Box 3255, Shortland St,
Auckland 1140, NZ or email: childrensbooks@hachette.co.nz

**Don't forget to include your name and address.
Only one entry per child.**

Good luck!

1. Ferno the Fire Dragon
2. Sepron the Sea Serpent
3. Arcta the Mountain Giant
4. Tagus the Horse-Man
5. Nanook the Snow Monster
6. Epos the Flame Bird

Beast Quest:
The Golden Armour
7. Zepha the Monster Squid
8. Claw the Giant Monkey
9. Soltra the Stone Charmer
10. Vipero the Snake Man
11. Arachnid the King of Spiders
12. Trillion the Three-Headed Lion

Beast Quest:
The Dark Realm
13. Torgor the Minotaur
14. Skor the Winged Stallion
15. Narga the Sea Monster
16. Kaymon the Gorgon Hound
17. Tusk the Mighty Mammoth
18. Sting the Scorpion Man

Beast Quest:
The Amulet of Avantia
19. Nixa the Death Bringer
20. Equinus the Spirit Horse
21. Rashouk the Cave Troll
22. Luna the Moon Wolf
23. Blaze the Ice Dragon
24. Stealth the Ghost Panther

Beast Quest:
The Shade of Death
25. Krabb Master of the Sea
26. Hawkite Arrow of the Air
27. Rokk the Walking Mountain
28. Koldo the Arctic Warrior
29. Trema the Earth Lord
30. Amictus the Bug Queen

Beast Quest:
The World of Chaos
31. Komodo the Lizard King
32. Muro the Rat Monster
33. Fang the Bat Fiend
34. Murk the Swamp Man
35. Terra Curse of the Forest
36. Vespick the Wasp Queen

Beast Quest:
The Lost World
37. Convol the Cold-Blooded Brute
38. Hellion the Fiery Foe
39. Krestor the Crushing Terror
40. Madara the Midnight Warrior
41. Ellik the Lightning Horror
42. Carnivora the Winged Scavenger

Beast Quest:
The Pirate King
- [ ] 43. Balisk the Water Snake
- [ ] 44. Koron Jaws of Death
- [ ] 45. Hecton the Body Snatcher
- [ ] 46. Torno the Hurricane Dragon
- [ ] 47. Kronus the Clawed Menace
- [ ] 48. Bloodboar the Buried Doom

Beast Quest:
The Warlock's Staff
- [ ] 49. Ursus the Clawed Roar
- [ ] 50. Minos the Demon Bull
- [ ] 51. Koraka the Winged Assassin
- [ ] 52. Silver the Wild Terror
- [ ] 53. Spikefin the Water King
- [ ] 54. Torpix the Twisting Serpent

Beast Quest:
Master of the Beasts
- [ ] 55. Noctila the Death Owl
- [ ] 56. Shamani the Raging Flame
- [ ] 57. Lustor the Acid Dart
- [ ] 58. Voltrex the Two-Headed Octopus
- [ ] 59. Tecton the Armoured Giant
- [ ] 60. Doomskull the King of Fear

Beast Quest:
The New Age
- [ ] 61. Elko Lord of the Sea
- [ ] 62. Tarrok the Blood Spike
- [ ] 63. Brutus the Hound of Horror
- [ ] 64. Flaymar the Scorched Blaze
- [ ] 65. Serpio the Slithering Shadow
- [ ] 66. Tauron the Pounding Fury

Beast Quest:
The Darkest Hour
- [ ] 67. Solak Scourge of the Sea
- [ ] 68. Kajin the Beast Catcher
- [ ] 69. Issrilla the Creeping Menace
- [ ] 70. Vigrash the Clawed Eagle
- [ ] 71. Mirka the Ice Horse
- [ ] 72. Kama the Faceless Beast

Special Bumper Editions
- [ ] Vedra & Krimon: Twin Beasts of Avantia
- [ ] Spiros the Ghost Phoenix
- [ ] Arax the Soul Stealer
- [ ] Kragos & Kildor: The Two-Headed Demon
- [ ] Creta the Winged Terror
- [ ] Mortaxe the Skeleton Warrior
- [ ] Ravira, Ruler of the Underworld
- [ ] Raksha the Mirror Demon
- [ ] Grashkor the Beast Guard
- [ ] Ferrok the Iron Soldier

All books priced at £4.99.
Special bumper editions priced at £5.99.

Orchard Books are available from all good bookshops, or can
be ordered from our website: www.orchardbooks.co.uk,
or telephone 01235 827702, or fax 01235 8227703.

Series 12: THE DARKEST HOUR
COLLECT THEM ALL!

Three lands are in terrible danger from six new
Beasts. Tom must ride to the rescue!

SOLAK
SCOURGE OF THE SEA

978 1 40832 396 0

KAJIN
THE BEAST CATCHER

978 1 40832 397 7

ISSRILLA
THE CREEPING MENACE

978 1 40832 398 4

VIGRASH
THE CLAWED EAGLE

978 1 40832 399 1

MIRKA
THE ICE HORSE

978 1 40832 400 4

KAMA
THE FACELESS BEAST

978 1 40832 401 1

Meet six terrifying new Beasts!

Skuric the Forest Demon
Targro the Arctic Menace
Slivka the Cold-hearted Curse
Linka the Sky Conqueror
Vermok the Spiteful Scavenger
Koba the Ghoul of the Shadows

SPECIAL BUMPER EDITION!

Watch out for the next Special Bumper Edition

Join Tom on his Beast Quests
and take part in a terrifying adventure
where YOU call the shots!

The Chronicles of Avantia

FROM THE DARK, A HERO ARISES...

Dare to enter the kingdom of Avantia.

A new evil arises in Avantia. Lord Derthsin has ordered his armies into the four corners of Avantia. If the four Beasts of Avantia can find their Chosen Riders they might have the strength to challenge Derthsin. But if they fail, the land of Avantia will be lost forever...

FIRST HERO, CHASING EVIL, CALL TO WAR, FIRE AND FURY- OUT NOW!

www.chroniclesofavantia.com

NEW ADAM BLADE SERIES

Coming soon 2013

Robobeasts battle in this deep sea cyber adventure.

Read on for an exclusive extract of
CEPHALOX THE CYBER SQUID!

THE MERRYN TOUCH

The water was up to Max's knees and still rising. Soon it would reach his waist. Then his chest. Then his face.

I'm going to die down here, he thought.

He hammered on the dome with all his strength, but the plexiglass held firm.

Then he saw something pale looming through the dark water outside the submersible. A long, silvery spike. It must be the squid-creature, with one of its weird robotic attachments. Any second now it would smash the glass and finish him off...

There was a crash. The sub rocked. The silver spike thrust through the broken plexiglass. More water surged in. Then the spike withdrew and the water poured in faster. Max forced his way against the torrent to the opening. If he could just squeeze through the gap...

The jet of water pushed him back. He took one last deep breath, and then the water was over his head.

He clamped his mouth shut, struggling forwards, feeling the pressure on his lungs build.

Something gripped his arms, but it wasn't the squid's tentacle – it was a pair of hands, pulling him through the hole. The broken plexiglass scraped his sides and then he was through.

The monster was nowhere to be seen. In the dim underwater light, he made out the face of his rescuer. It was the Merryn girl, and next to her was a large silver swordfish.

She smiled at him.

Max couldn't smile back. He'd been saved from a metal coffin, only to swap it for a watery one. The pressure of the ocean squeezed him on every side. His lungs felt as

———

though they were bursting.

He thrashed his limbs, rising upwards. He looked to where he thought the surface was, but saw nothing, only endless water. His cheeks puffed with the effort to hold in air. He let some of it out slowly, but it only made him want to breathe in more.

He knew he had no chance. He was too deep, he'd never make it to the surface in time. Soon he'd no longer be able to hold his breath. The water would swirl into his lungs and he'd die here, at the bottom of the sea. *Just like my mother*, he thought.

The Merryn girl rose up beside him, reached out and put her hands on his neck. Warmth seemed to flow from her fingers. Then the warmth turned to pain. What was happening? It got worse and worse, until Max felt as if his throat was being ripped open. Was she trying to kill him?

———

He struggled in panic, trying to push her off. His mouth opened and water rushed in.

That was it. He was going to die.

Then he realised something – the water was cool and sweet. He sucked it down into his lungs. Nothing had ever tasted so good.

He was breathing underwater!

He put his hands to his neck and found two soft, gill-like openings where the Merryn girl had touched him. His eyes widened in astonishment.

The girl smiled.

Other strange things were happening. Max found he could see more clearly. The water seemed lighter and thinner. He made out the shapes of underwater plants, rock formations and shoals of fish in the distance, which had been invisible before. And he didn't feel as if the ocean was crushing him any more.

Is this what it's like to be a Merryn? he wondered.

"I'm Lia," said the girl. "And this is Spike." She patted the swordfish on the back and it nuzzled against her.

"Hi, I'm Max." He clapped his hand to his mouth in shock. He was speaking the same strange language of sighs and whistles he'd heard the girl use when he first met her – but now it made sense, as if he was born to speak it.

"What have you done to me?" he said.

"Saved your life," said Lia. "You're welcome, by the way."

"Oh – don't think I'm not grateful – I am. But – you've turned me into a Merryn?"

The girl laughed. "Not exactly, but I've given you some Merryn powers. You can breathe underwater, speak our language, and your senses are much stronger. Come on – we need to get away from here. The Cyber Squid may come back."

In one graceful movement she slipped onto Spike's back. Max clambered on behind her.

"Hold tight," Lia said. "Spike – let's go!"

Max put his arms around the Merryn's waist. He was jerked backwards as the swordfish shot off through the water, but he managed to hold on.

They raced above underwater forests of gently waving fronds, and hills and valleys of rock. Max saw giant crabs scuttling over the seabed. Undersea creatures loomed up – jellyfish, an octopus, a school of dolphins – but Spike nimbly swerved round them.

"Where are we going?" Max asked.

"You'll see," Lia said over her shoulder.

"I need to find my dad," Max said. The crazy things that had happened in the last few moments had driven his father from his mind. Now it all came flooding back. Was his dad gone for good? "We have to do something! That monster's got my dad – and my dogbot too!"

"It's not the Cyber Squid who wants your father. It's the Professor who's *controlling* the Cyber Squid. I tried to warn you back at the city – but you wouldn't listen."

"I didn't understand you then!"

"You Breathers don't try to understand – that's your whole problem!"

"I'm trying now. What is that monster? And who is the Professor?"

"I'll explain everything when we arrive."

"Arrive where?"

The seabed suddenly fell away. A steep valley sloped down, leading way, way deeper than the ocean ridge Aquora was built on. The swordfish dived. The water grew darker.

Far below, Max saw a faint yellow glimmer. As he watched it grew bigger and brighter, until it became a vast undersea city of golden-glinting rock rushing up towards them. There were towers, spires, domes, bridges, courtyards, squares, gardens. A city as big as Aquora, and far more beautiful, at the bottom of the sea.

———

Max gasped in amazement. The water was
dark, but the city emitted a glow of its own
– a warm phosphorescent light that spilled
from the many windows. The rock sparkled.

Orange, pink and scarlet corals and seashells decorated the walls in intricate patterns.

"This is – amazing!" he said.

Lia turned round and smiled at him. "It's my home," she said. "Sumara!"

LOOK OUT FOR SERIES 5:
THE CHAOS QUADRANT

SYTHID
THE SPIDER CRAB

978 1 40833 471 3

BRUX
THE TUSKED TERROR

978 1 40833 471 3

VENOR
THE SEA SCORPION

978 1 40833 475 1

MONOTH
THE SPIKED DESTROYER

978 1 40833 477 5

DON'T MISS THE NEXT SPECIAL
BUMPER EDITION: OCTOR,
MONSTER OF THE DEEP!